Have You Ever Seen...?

for Joey

First published 1986

Ashton Scholastic Limited
165 Marua Road, Panmure, PO Box 12328, Auckland 6, New Zealand.

Ashton Scholastic Pty Limited
PO Box 579, Gosford, NSW 2250, Australia.

Scholastic Publications Ltd
Holly Walk, Leamington Spa, Warwickshire CV32 4LS, England.

Scholastic Inc.
730 Broadway, New York NY 10003, USA.

Scholastic-TAB Publications Ltd
123 Newkirk Road, Richmond Hill, Ontario L4C 3G5, Canada.

Copyright © John Tarlton, 1985

National Library of New Zealand Cataloguing-in-Publication data

TARLTON, John.
   Have you ever seen— / written and illustrated by John Tarlton. — Auckland, N.Z.: Ashton Scholastic, 1986. — 1 v. — (Read by reading)
   Children's story.
   ISBN 0-908643-47-0
      428.6 (NZ823.2)
1. Readers (Elementary).
I. Title. II. Series.

5432   789/8

Typeset in Souvenir by Rennies Illustrations Ltd

Printed in Hong Kong

Have You Ever Seen....?

John Tarlton

READ BY READING
Ashton Scholastic
Auckland   New York   London   Toronto   Sydney

Have you ever seen . . .

a rat bike riding

or a lion sled sliding

or a cat stamp licking

or a dog tune picking

or a camel ice skating

or a panda hook baiting

or a turtle pot throwing

or a monkey glass blowing

or a rabbit book reading

or a walrus dough kneading

or an elephant sun tanning

or a pelican house planning

or a rhinoceros singing a sweet refrain

or a hippopotamus dusting pink porcelain?

If you haven't seen such sights before

and you'd like to see some more . . .

then find a pen and paper
and see what *you* can draw!

21